HANNAH

Disney's
EASY
TO
READ
STORIES

A Collection of Six Favorite Tales

A
MOUSE WORKS
STORYBOOK COLLECTION

"Toy Story: Buzz and the Bubble Planet" is based on the original story
Toy Story: Buzz and the Bubble Planet, illustrated by Sol Studios.
"Aladdin: Abu Monkeys Around" is based on the original story
Aladdin: Abu Monkeys Around, illustrated by Darren Hont.
"The Lion King: Roar" is based on the original story
The Lion King: Roar, illustrated by Adam Devancy and Darren Hont.
"Lady and the Tramp: What's That Noise?" is based on the original story
Lady and the Tramp: What's That Noise?, illustrated by Sol Studios.
"Mulan: Lost" is based on the original story *Mulan: Lost*, illustrated by
Denise Shimabukuro, Korey Heinzen, Anna Leong, and Woody Herman.
"The Little Mermaid: Ariel and the Very Best Book" is based on the original story
The Little Mermaid: Ariel and the Very Best Book, illustrated by Sol Studios.

CONTENTS

BUZZ AND THE BUBBLE PLANET

by Judy Katschke

There was a new toy in Andy's room.
"It looks like a spaceship,"
said Woody.
"Did you say 'spaceship'?"
Buzz asked.

Buzz got in the spaceship.

Woody told Buzz to be careful.

Buzz was ready to blast off.

"Buzz, don't go!" Woody said.

Uh-oh!

Woody hit the 'on' switch.

Whoosh!
The spaceship went
up, up, and away!
Then it came down.
Buzz fell out.

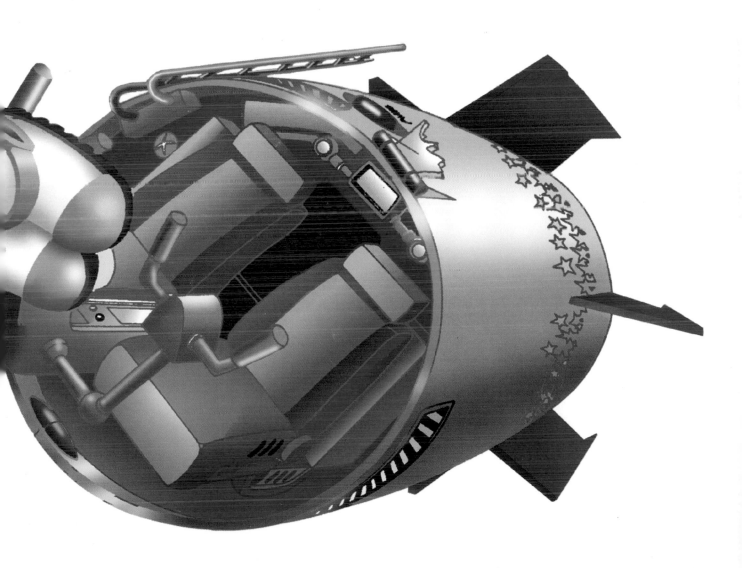

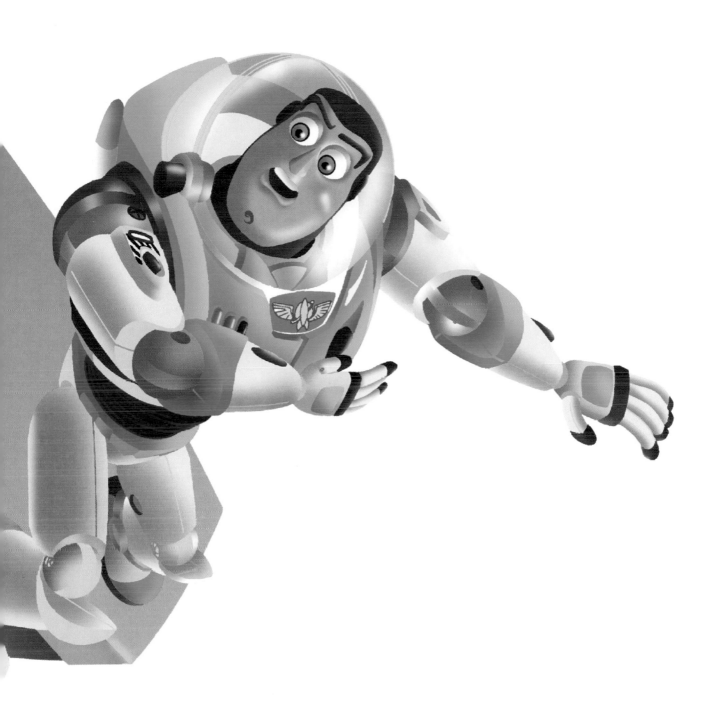

Buzz landed in some water.

He jumped out.

The water went down.

"I am on a strange planet,"
said Buzz.
"I must look around.
After all, I *am* Buzz Lightyear!
But how will I get home?"
he said.

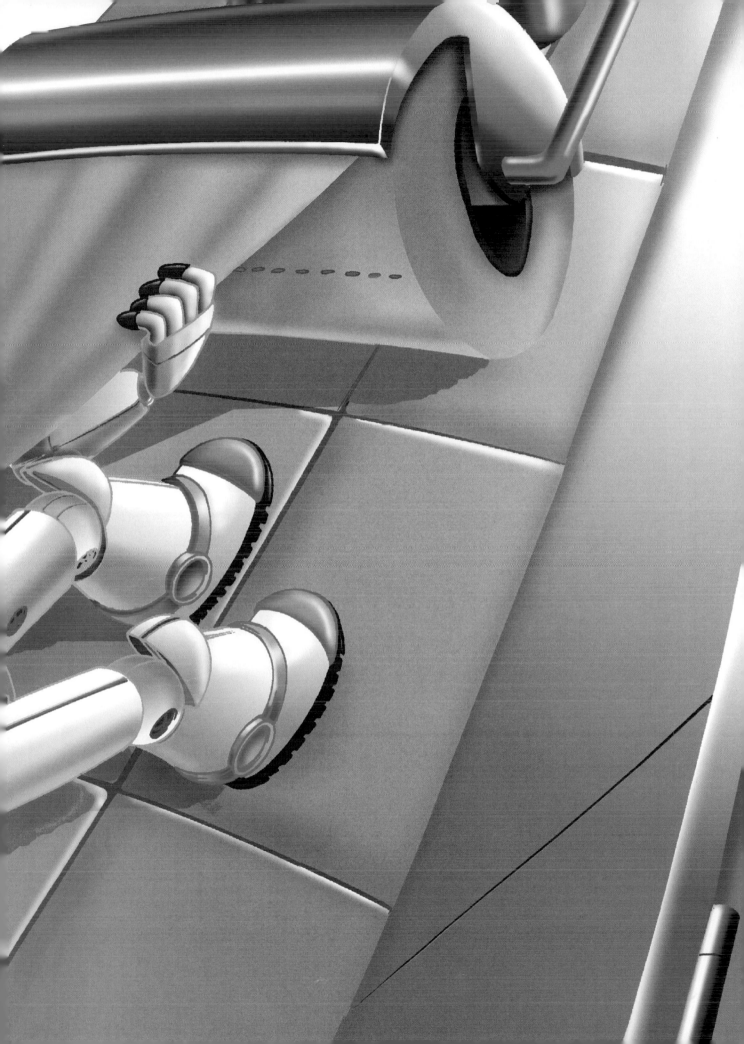

Back in Andy's room,
the toys held a meeting.
"We must find Buzz," said Woody.
"I will send out
the green army men," said Sarge.
"Great idea!" said the toys.

Buzz was in trouble.

A robot was pushing him.

It shook in his hands.

Buzz could not hold on.

Buzz hit a button.

The robot stopped.

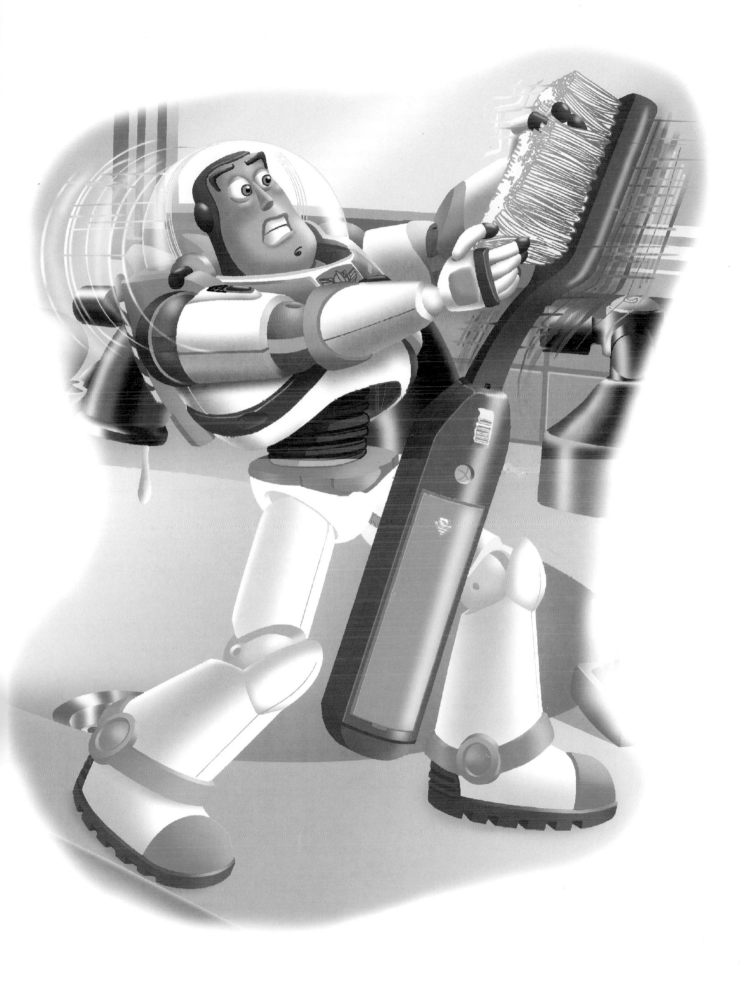

Next, strong winds
pushed Buzz.

He slipped on a rock.

He was covered in blue slime.

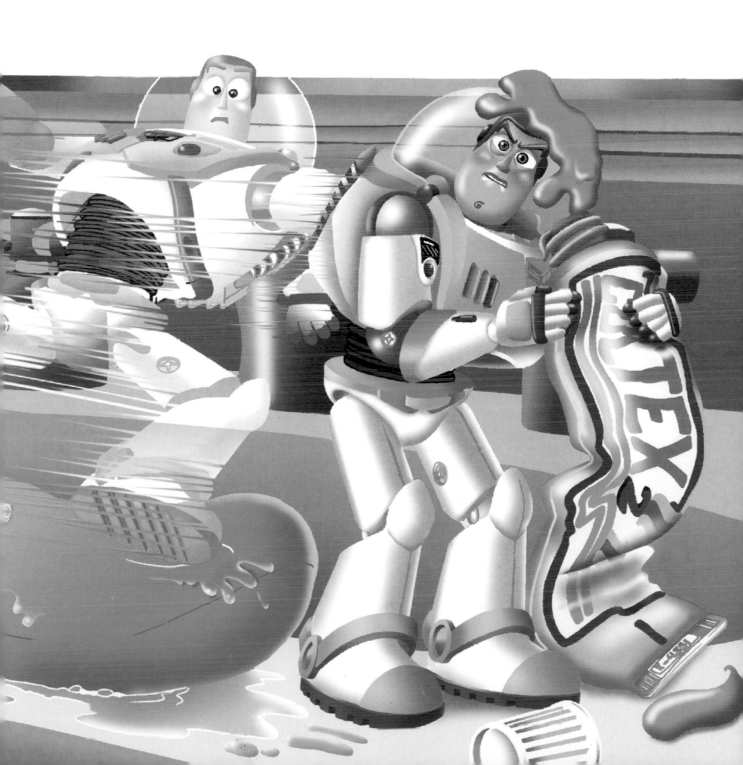

Buzz saw Andy's cat,
Whiskers.

"Do not worry, Whiskers.

I will rescue you," said Buzz.

The cat's tail swung at Buzz.

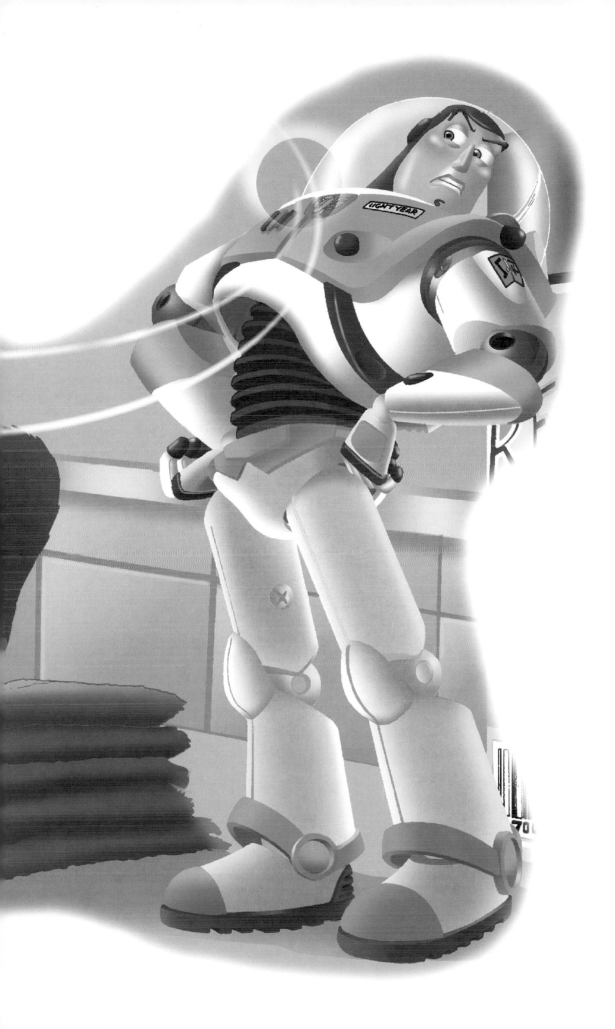

THUMP!

Buzz was in a red boat.

"This planet moves

too much," said Buzz.

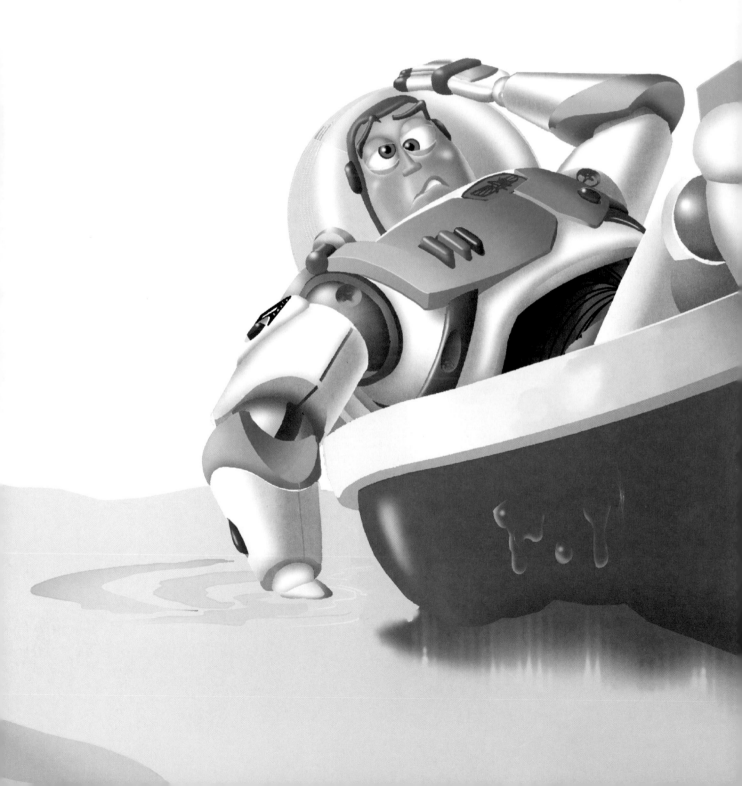

Buzz saw yellow aliens.

They swam to him.

"Who is your leader?"

Buzz called.

"Squeak," said the yellow aliens.

Buzz's wings opened.

His wings hit a bottle of
SQUEAKY-CLEAN BUBBLES.

"You must be Squeak," Buzz said.

"I am Buzz Lightyear. I come in peace."

Thick pink goo
came out of Squeak's head.
The goo turned into lots of bubbles.
Buzz slapped the bubbles.
But they were all around him.

Sarge and his men saw Buzz.

Sarge called Woody.

"Should we save him?" he asked.

"Do not worry," said Woody.

"Help is on the way!"

Back on the Bubble Planet,
Buzz was in trouble again.
Aliens were all around him.
Soon he would fall
into Squeak's bubble trap.

At last, help came.

Andy was on the Bubble Planet.

And Andy had Woody.

"Let's go, partners!" Andy said.

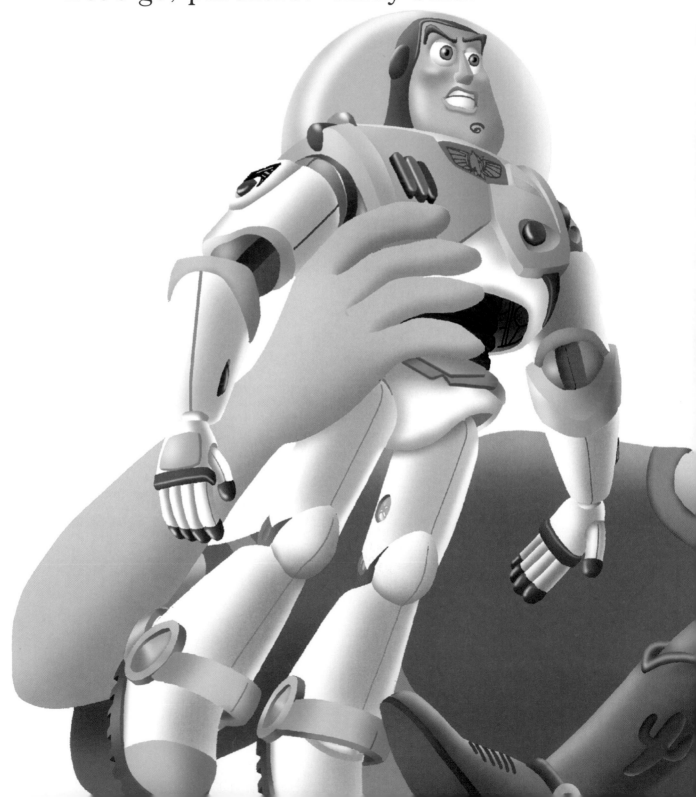

The Bubble Planet was
not so scary anymore.
Buzz was happy.
His friends were here.
And he was clean!

DISNEY'S

THE
LION KING

ROAR!

by Patricia Grossman

The day begins.

Simba and Nala say hello.

Then they start to roar.

Simba roars at the tall giraffes.

The giraffes chew the grass.

They toss their heads.

Nala roars at the monkeys.

They are busy.

The monkeys just laugh at Nala.

Simba roars at the big elephants.

They are not afraid.

The elephants just trumpet back.

Nala roars at the zebras.

The zebras do not look up.

They just keep eating.

Simba and Nala see Zazu.
Zazu is napping high in a tree.
Now Simba and Nala
can have some fun!

Simba roars at Zazu.

Simba's roar is loud!

Zazu keeps napping.

He does not hear Simba.

Nala roars at Zazu.

Nala's roar is loud!

Zazu does not hear Nala, either.

He just keeps dreaming.

Simba roars louder at Zazu.

Zazu still does not wake up.

He just snores.

Simba and Nala look at each other.

Then they look at Zazu.

At last they *both* roar at Zazu.

Their roar is very loud!

Good-bye, nap.

Good-bye, dreams.

Good-bye, snores.

"Go roar somewhere else!"

shouts Zazu.

Nala and Simba just laugh!

Aladdin
Abu Monkeys Around

by Anne Schreiber

From Monday,
when the week began,
to Sunday, at its end,
Abu played tricks on the Genie
and all of the Genie's friends.

On Monday,

everyone was sleeping.

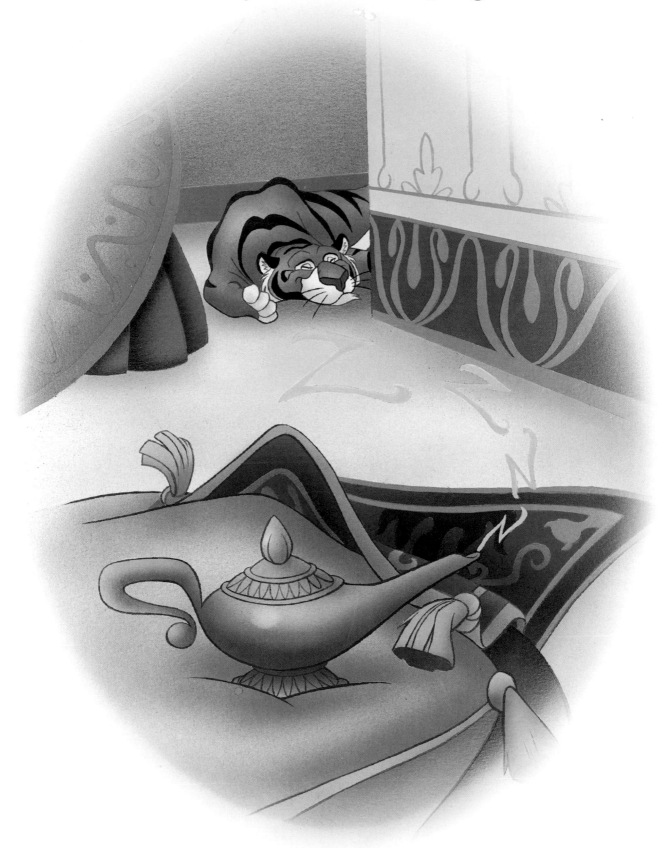

Except Abu.

BANG!

Abu banged the lamp.

It started to shake.

It fell on the floor.

Is the Genie awake?

On Tuesday,

the Genie was combing.

But not Abu.

CLANG!

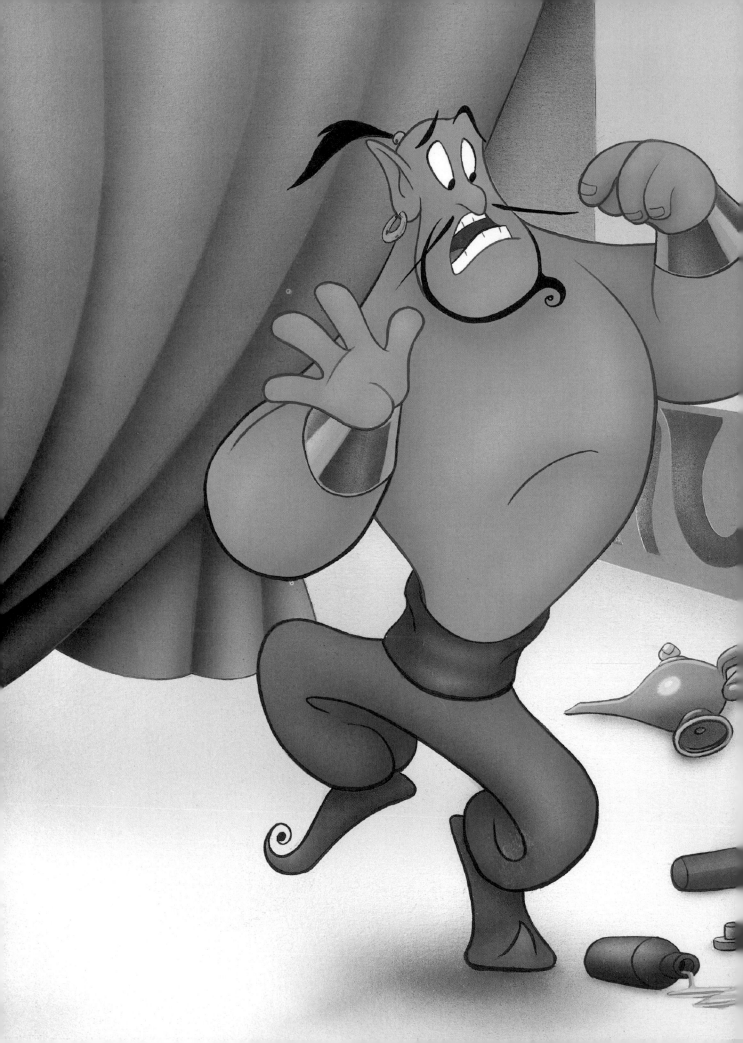

Abu scared the Genie
by ringing a bell.
The Genie jumped up.
Down Abu fell.

On Wednesday,
everyone was eating.

Except Abu.

CRASH!

Abu spilled the juice.

He dropped the fruit.

The Genie got juice
all over his suit.

On Thursday,

everyone was resting.

Except Abu.

SPLASH!

Abu jumped into the water.

He wanted to swim.

Aladdin got wet.

The Genie fell in.

On Friday,

everyone was shopping.

Except Abu.

WHOOSH!

Abu left a mess
on the ground.
His friends walked by
and slid all around.

On Saturday,

everyone was working.

Except Abu.

SWOOSH!

Abu jumped up
to grab a sweet treat.
He knocked a basket over.
Apples rolled down the street.

What has Abu done?

On Monday he woke the Genie.

On Tuesday he made things crash.

On Wednesday he spilled the juice.

On Thursday he made a splash.

On Friday he left a mess,

and all his friends fell down.

On Saturday he jumped on a fruit stand,

and spilled apples on the ground.

On Sunday, when the
week was through,
no one could sleep.

Except Abu.

ZZZZZZZZZZZ.

Disney's
Lady and the TRAMP

What's That Noise?

by Carol Pugliano-Martin

It was a dark night.
Lady and Tramp were alone
in the house.
Suddenly, Lady heard a noise.

"What's that noise?" Lady asked Tramp.

"The floor is making that noise,"
said Tramp.

Lady was not so sure.

But Tramp said,

"Lady, we are safe and sound.

I am the bravest dog around!"

Tramp shut his eyes.

But Lady could not sleep.

"I must watch the house!"
she said.

Then Lady heard another noise.

She shook Tramp.

"What's that noise?" Lady asked.

"That noise is just the wind,"
said Tramp.
"Lady, we are safe and sound.
I am the bravest dog around!"

Lady heard another noise!

Bang! Crash!

Who was outside the house?

"What's that noise?"
Lady asked Tramp.
Tramp said,
"That is just thunder.
Lady, we are safe and sound.
I am the bravest dog around!"

"I hope you are right," Lady said.

Lady heard another sound.

Plink! Plink!

Was there someone *inside* the house?

Lady ran to the kitchen
and barked.
Tramp ran in.

"What's that noise?" Lady asked.
"That noise is the rain
falling into the pot," Tramp said.

Tramp said,

"Lady, we are safe and sound.

I am the bravest dog around!"

Lady heard the windows shake.

Then she heard a loud bark.

"Ruff! Ruff! Ruff!"

It was Tramp!

Tramp was looking at
a big shadow on the wall.
"What is that?" Tramp asked Lady.
Lady had to find out what it was.

Lady said, "I must be brave."
She looked at the rug.
The big shadow was
a teeny, tiny bug!

Tramp was still on the piano.

"Do not be afraid," Lady said.

"It is a teeny, tiny bug."

"I was not afraid," Tramp said.

"Tramp, you were right," Lady said.

"We *are* safe and sound."

"That's right," Tramp said.

"We are the bravest dogs around!"

DISNEY'S
MULAN
Lost!

by Kathryn Cristaldi McKeon

Mulan was hot and tired.

She was a soldier.

It was hard work.

Yao made fun of Mulan.
"That skinny guy is
one strange bird," he said.
Ling and Chien-Po laughed.

Mulan, Yao, Ling, and Chien-Po
shot arrows.

They needed to practice.

Mulan shot an arrow at a tree.

TWANG!

The arrow came
very close to Yao's hair.

"I guess my aim is a little off,"
Mulan said in a deep voice.

Yao's face was red.

He grabbed Mulan's arrow.

He shot the arrow into the woods.

"You'd better get that," Yao told Mulan.

"You need more practice."

"Wait for me," Mulan said.

"We will wait here," they said.

Mulan and Mushu
walked into the woods.
They walked for a long time.
They did not see the arrow.
Mushu was worried.
"Where are we?" he asked.

Mulan looked to the right.

She looked to the left.

She called her friends.

But no one answered.

"We are lost!" said Mushu.

Mushu leaned back on a tree.

The tree was soft and warm.

The tree was furry!

"Hey, this tree is not a tree!" said Mushu.

"No, it is a giant panda bear!"
Mulan cried.
"Help!" said Mushu.

Mulan saw a bamboo tree.

She grabbed some leaves.

Panda bears love bamboo leaves.

He sat down and ate them.

Mulan and Mushu were still lost.
"Maybe this swamp meets up
with the lake near our camp," said Mulan.
Mushu climbed onto a log.

"Mushu," said Mulan.
"That log has a lot of teeth."
Mushu was standing
on a giant alligator!
"Aaaah!" he screamed.

"Help!" Mushu shouted.
Mulan grabbed some reeds.
She waved the reeds in the air.
"You are getting very sleepy,"
she told the alligator.

The alligator fell asleep.

"I was getting dizzy," said Mushu.

"I knew you were a dizzy dragon!"
Mulan said.

Mulan and Mushu were still lost.

"Where is our camp?" asked Mushu.

"I think I can see it," said Mulan.

When they got close to the camp
they heard crying and snarling.
Yao, Ling, and Chien-Po were
surrounded by wolves.
The wolves were snarling.
The men were crying.

"Good-bye, world!" said Chien-Po.

Yao covered his eyes.

"I want my mommy!" said Ling.

Mulan had an idea.

She hid behind a tree.

"Aaaooo!" she cried. *"Aaaooo!"*

The wolves howled at the moon.

The men walked away.

They did not see Mulan.

Back at camp Yao told their story.
"A pack of monster wolves
surrounded us," he said.
"But we showed them
who was boss," said Ling.

"You guys are so brave," Mulan said.
"Those wolves would make me
cry for my mommy."
Then she smiled at Mushu.

DISNEY'S THE LITTLE MERMAID
Ariel and the Very Best Book

by Patrick Daley and Joan Michael

"Where is Ariel?"
asked the King of the Sea.
Sebastian said,
"She is reading again.
Come with us
and you will see."

King Triton scolded Ariel.
"Why must you read
all day and all night?
Books are for people.
This just is not right."

"But, Father, I will show you
how great books can be.
I will show you my best books.
Then you will see."

"Look, Father, look.
Look at this book.
It has pictures and maps
and places to go.
There are wonderful places.
These are places to know."

King Triton frowned.

"A book full of maps?

That is no good to me.

I have no need for maps.

I live in the sea!"

Ariel tried again.

"Look at this book.

It is full of fish.

It tells all about them.

It tells all you wish."

"A book about fish?
That is no good to me.
I know all about fish,"
said the King of the Sea.

"I will find you a book,"
Ariel said with a smile.
"I will find a book.
But it may take a while."

"I will draw and I will write.
I will cut and I will color.

I will make him a book
that is like no other."

Said the King of the Sea,
"What is this book
you are giving to me?
It tells all about
our life in the sea!
Yes, this is a good book.
I have to agree."

"It is the very best book,"
said the King of the Sea.
"Would you like to read it?
Would you read it to me?"